Albert the Dragon

Albert the Dragon

ROSEMARY WEIR

ILLUSTRATED BY QUENTIN BLAKE

ABELARD-SCHUMAN

LONDON NEW YORK TORONTO

LONDON
Abelard-Schuman
Limited
8 King Street

NEW YORK
Abelard-Schuman
Limited
6 West 57 Street

TORONTO
Abelard-Schuman
Canada Limited
81 John Street

© *Rosemary Weir* 1961
Library of Congress Catalogue Card Number 60: 13631
First published 1961

Contents

U. S. 1160289

Albert tries to help

A very long time ago, before the days of trains and planes, dragons lived in Cornwall, on the most southwestern tip of England. They lived in caves among the rocks, and people found them rather a nuisance because they were so big. When they got excited they breathed out fire and smoke, and this set heather and ferns alight and caused fires just where the farmers didn't want them. Then too, they used to carry off sheep for their dinner, and some people believed they took children also. Whether this was true or not, it was a very useful thing to threaten children with, and parents used to say: " If you don't behave yourself the dragons'll get you! "

Now, just outside the little village of Tregunna Cove, there lived one particular dragon called Albert. And he hated to hear people tell their children " the dragon'll get you " because, in his case at least, it simply wasn't true. Albert was particularly fond of children, and he certainly wouldn't have eaten

7

them, because he happened to be a vegetarian, and only ate grass and small trees, and sometimes seaweed for a change.

It was a great grief to Albert that he was never able to make friends with any of the children from Tregunna Cove because, none of them being particularly good children, they all ran away screaming as soon as he approached. He used to spend hours lying on the rocks outside his cave watching the children playing in the village far below, and wondering how he could make them understand he meant them no harm. But dragons, although large animals, had very small brains, so he never got any further than saying to himself, in a rather whining voice:

"I *wish* they'd be friends. I wish they'd come and play. I'd love to invite a nice little girl to tea, or even a nice little boy. We could play bonfires, all children like that, and it's one of the few things I'm really good at. I *wish* they'd be friends–" and then he'd start all over again.

One night, about nine o'clock, Albert was wandering on the moor outside the village when he saw a light in the downstairs window of a farmhouse. He knew the farm because a small boy called Tony lived there, and the dragon had often thought that he looked a nice boy, just the sort of boy who ought to enjoy playing bonfires with a dragon. So he thought to himself: "I'll go, very quietly, and listen outside

8

that window, and perhaps I may be able to pick up some idea as to why people hate dragons so much, and what I could do to make them understand I want to be friends." So he slithered very quietly over the ground until he arrived at the lighted window and then he lay still and listened. But the window was tightly shut, and he could hear no more than a murmur of voices. Albert got very worried, and he started to pant, and wriggle, and got hotter and hotter until steam began to puff out of his nostrils.

Inside the room the farmer's wife said to her husband:

" 'Tis tarrible close all of a sudden! I can hardly breathe, I do declare. Open the window, Tony my boy, and let in a breath of air! "

Tony crossed to the window and flung it open, so that the dragon, crouching down and trying hard not to breathe, could hear everything that was said in the room.

" I must keep *cool*," he told himself, and gradually he managed to choke down the flames which threatened to burst from his nostrils, and the steam blew away into the cold air.

Inside the house the family was getting ready for bed.

" Go you on up, Tony," said the farmer's wife. " There's one or two things I must do before I goes to bed."

9

" I've locked the door," said the farmer.

" Well then you can just unlock 'un agin, because I've not put out the bowl of cream for the pixie. My dear life! How do 'ee think I'd get on without the pixie to lend me a hand, and he won't work without his drop o' cream, as you do know well enough, *and* the door left left ajar for 'im to come in."

Albert, crouching in the darkness, heard the door unlocked, and a chinking noise as a dish was set down on the step. Then the light went out, and the footsteps of Mr and Mrs Farmer went upstairs to bed. He was extremely interested in what he heard about the pixie and the cream. He knew the pixies of course, everyone did, and pesky little bothersome creatures he'd always thought them. He'd certainly never known before that they were prepared to help humans with their work in return for a bowl of cream!

Albert decided to stay and watch. Perhaps, he thought, if he could discover what it was the pixies did, he could do it too, and then the humans would be grateful to *him* and give *him* bowls of cream, and let their little girls and boys come to tea and play bonfires. So Albert settled himself comfortably for the night, with one eye shut to sleep, and the other open to keep watch, which is a useful accomplishment dragons happen to have.

Dawn was breaking when the pixie came at last.

He came so silently Albert wouldn't have heard him if he hadn't happened to chink the bowl of cream when he set it down after drinking. Albert was wide awake in a minute. He lifted his head, very cautiously, and looked in through the kitchen window. There was the pixie, as busy as a bee! First, he lit the fire, and swept the hearth clean. Next he swept the floor, dusted everything nicely, set the chairs straight, laid the table for breakfast, and then, putting a big black pot on the now roaring fire he proceeded to make the porridge. This done, the pixie gave a last look round to see everything was in order and vanished as silently as he had come. No sooner was he out of the room than down came the farmer and his wife and after them, yawning and stretching, came Tony.

The farmer's wife began to praise the pixie.

"The dear liddle fellow! Whatever would I do without him! Everything so clean and nice and the porridge made just right! He's worth his drop o' cream and more, so 'ee be!"

Albert, listening outside the window, was very jealous.

"Nothing there I couldn't do. Lot of fuss about a few simple little jobs!" And he began to get so heated that steam poured from his nostrils and clouded the kitchen window.

"Proper misty ol' day," said the farmer, and Al-

11

bert, horrified at what he had done, wriggled away and went back to his cave to think things out.

Next morning very early, before it was light, the dragon was back at the farm. He saw with satisfaction that the bowl of cream was on the step, untouched, which meant the pixie had not yet arrived. So, very carefully, he slithered through the door and into the farmhouse kitchen. It was a tight fit but he managed it.

"Fire first," he muttered to himself, and he found a heap of dry sticks all ready for the fire and piled them on the hearth. Then he puffed and puffed and worked himself up until he felt really warm and a thin spurt of flame shot out of either nostril. The fire burned beautifully and Albert was delighted.

"Now sweep and dust," he told himself, and he crept round the room, carefully puffing and blowing into all the corners until he raised a cloud of dust which he blew before him out of the back door. The room looked spotless. Pixies indeed! What could pixies do that dragons couldn't do better?

Now the porridge! He filled the big iron pot from the water bucket and hung it on a hook over the bright fire. And then he paused; he couldn't remember what it was the pixie had put into the pot to make the porridge!

He was so worried he couldn't keep cool, and a nasty little smell of singeing began to rise from the

12

hearthrug where he sat. He moved quickly off the rug, and as he did, the end of his tail caught a row of plates on the shelf and swept them all to the floor! The noise was terrific, and just as poor Albert escaped into the darkness of the farmyard, the

farmer and his wife came rushing down the stairs.

The farmer's wife surveyed the ruins of her best china. "It's that pesky cat! Oh, what won't I do to 'er when I catch 'er!" But then she caught sight of the lighted fire, and the pot put on to boil, and stopped in amazement.

"It's never the pixie," she said, and she went to

13

the door and glanced outside. "No, it's not 'im, cream's still there. Besides 'e'd never break my plates. Husband, what's been going on? I don't like this at all!"

"Look here," said the farmer, and he pointed to the floor. Poor Albert, in his hurry to escape, had knocked over the flour barrel, and there, plainly showing in the spilt flour, was the unmistakable print of a dragon's foot!

"Dragons, is it?" cried the farmer's wife in a rage. "I'll give 'em dragons! Coming here and messin' up my kitchen!"

"Mother, *please* don't be cross," said Tony.

"And why not indeed?"

"Because the poor old dragon was only trying to help. We all have accidents sometimes. You know you broke the best blue vase yourself week before last. I'm sure this dragon is a *good* dragon. He wanted to help, like the pixie, but he just didn't know how. Mother, he must be feeling *awfully* sad and disappointed." And Tony's eyes filled with tears at the thought of the dragon's grief.

The farmer's wife fumbled for her handkerchief, but of course being in her nightie she couldn't find it.

"You'll make me cry, you and your sorrowful dragons! Oh well, we'll say no more about it, but come daylight Tony, you'll go out and find that dragon and tell him we don't want any more of his sort of help. Say it nicely, but be firm Tony! Now what's the matter with *you?*" she demanded, turning on her husband, who was clearing his throat and blowing his nose loudly on a red bandanna handkerchief.

"Nothing really. Just sorry for the old chap—trying to help, and getting in this mess. After all, housework isn't the job for dragons. Tell him Tony, when you go, that if he likes to come up along and give me a hand to burn the old ferns on Top Pasture, I'll be glad of his help."

Later that day Tony set out in search of the dragon. He had no difficulty in finding where Albert lived because all the way up the hillside to the cave there were large white floury footsteps. Albert was lying in front of his cave. His eyes were red, and he was still sniffing unhappily. A very little, rather damp steam rose from his nostrils into the warm, sunny air.

Tony sat down on a rock beside the dragon.

"Hullo," he said.

"Hul-hullo."

"Don't cry old chap, it's all right, honestly it is."

The dragon looked up at the little boy, and a ray of hope showed in his swollen eyes.

"All *right?* But – but – aren't your parents simply furious – I mean about the frightful mess I made of things?"

"They understand," said Tony, and he told the dragon all that his mother and father had said.

Albert jumped to his feet, "But that's *wonderful!* Help your father burn the ferns? Of course I will. Delighted, old chap! Any little thing I can do to help!" And then he stopped and said, very shyly,

"I say!"

"Yes?"

"I wonder if you'd care – now say at once if you wouldn't, but I *wonder* if you'd care to – to come to tea?"

" Why, I'd *love* it," said Tony.

" We could play bonfires! " suggested Albert happily and he blew a great jet of orange flame out of his nose!

Albert and the Valiant Knight

One fine summer day, a very long time ago, Albert the dragon was lying on a flat slab of rock in front of his cave, drowsing in the sun. He was almost asleep when a curious clanking sound came to his ears, and he looked up lazily to discover what could be causing it. He saw a Knight, all shining in the sun, wearing helmet and breastplate, carrying a shield and riding a huge black horse. The Knight was some little way off, travelling across the bare, rocky countryside towards a castle set on the cliffs overlooking the sea.

"Going on a visit I suppose," thought Albert sleepily. "Nice shiny suit that, though not as nice as mine." And he rippled the scales on his back so that they changed from green to blue, which is a thing dragons can do quite easily. "Bet he can't blow fire through his nostrils either," thought Albert. "Oh well, I daresay he's all right as far as he goes. We can't all be dragons." And Albert stretched himself out once more and fell fast asleep.

He was wakened an hour later by the sound of someone hurrying up the steep path which led from the village to his cave.

"It's Tony!" thought Albert with pleasure. "I'm glad he's come, now we'll have some fun!"

But Tony, when at last he arrived panting on the rock beside Albert, didn't look at all like someone who had come to have fun. He looked a very worried little boy indeed.

"Albert!" he exclaimed. "Something terrible has happened!"

"Sorry to hear that, old chap," said Albert. "Very sorry. Anything I can do to help?"

"It's *you* who'll want help!" said Tony.

"Me? But nothing terrible has happened to me!"

"No, but it's going to, if we don't do something about it. Oh Albert, I don't know how to tell you—!"

"Let's just sit down quietly, shall we?" said Albert. "And take it steady. That's right. Now don't cry, old chap–not that you would, of course, but still –don't. Now then, what's the trouble?"

"It's the Knight!" burst out Tony.

"Oh, the Knight. Yes, I saw him pass. Going to spend the weekend at the castle I fancy. You mustn't let him frighten you, old boy."

"I'm *not* frightened!" said Tony indignantly.

19

"At least I am a bit, but for *you*, not me. You see, that Knight–I've heard of him before, everyone's talking about him–he's come down here to-to kill dragons! "

"Goodness me," said Albert mildly. " Now, why should he want to do that? "

"Well," said Tony. "You know yourself, Albert, most dragons aren't as well-behaved as you are. They *do* rampage about and eat sheep and–and children sometimes–"

"Rubbish! " said Albert.

"Well, it may be rubbish, but everyone believes it. And this Knight has sworn to wipe out all the dragons in Cornwall. He's been down in the village asking people all sorts of questions–how many children have been eaten, and things like that–and he's promised them a perfectly wonderful fight between himself and–and you."

" *Me?* " said Albert. "But that's ridiculous! I'm not going to fight him or anyone. And I never ate a child in my life, they can't truthfully say I did. You know very well I'm a vegetarian."

"I *know*," said Tony. "Everyone knows that. But you see the trouble is that they all want to see the fight. They're planning to make a public holiday of it, and have refreshments and side shows and things, just like a fair."

"Well, I think they might have asked me first,"

20

said Albert grumpily. " Now they'll be disappointed because it isn't coming off, and they'll blame me."

" Yes," said Tony. " I'm afraid they will. And it's worse than that, Albert, because the Knight says he'll force you to fight. He says he knows ways of bringing dragons into the open when they hide in their caves and don't want to fight."

"Oh, he does, does he? " said Albert thoughtfully. " What sort of ways? "

" I only wish I knew," said Tony gloomily, and for some minutes the two of them sat in silence, thinking hard.

At last Albert said : " This fellow, this Knight, is he a decent sort of chap? "

" Yes, I think he is, except about killing dragons," said Tony.

" Well, look here, I've got an idea. You go and talk to him, Tony. Tell him I'm–er–" Albert wriggled shyly–" tell him I'm not a bad sort of chap, and that I don't eat anything except grass and small trees and sometimes seaweed. Explain to him that the people here don't really want me killed, they only want the fun of watching a fight. Tell him all that and then see if you can't come to some arrangement with him."

" What sort of arrangement? " asked Tony.

" Well–you know. I'll fight him if he promises not to hurt me. I'll even let him win."

" But Albert, don't you see, if he wins he'll have to cut off your head ! "

" Oh, I don't think so," said Albert, " no, I really don't think there is any need of that. I can roll over on my back, and he can put the point of his sword on my throat–only carefully, because I'm very ticklish –and then you can beg him to spare my life and he can graciously consent. It ought to go rather well. I shall quite enjoy it."

" But suppose he won't agree? " asked Tony doubtfully.

" Oh, he'll agree all right. Why shouldn't he? After all, he's to win, and he mightn't win, you know, if we really fought properly. I'm a very powerful dragon." Albert reflectively rippled his scales and blew a little smoke out of his nose. " Tell him he shall have the whole works if he agrees, green fire, smoke, tail lashing, everything. We'll keep it up for about an hour and a half and I'll gradually get weaker and weaker and then just roll over with my eyes half shut and my claws all limp, like this." And Albert rolled over and looked so dead that Tony was quite alarmed.

" Then," said Albert, turning right side up again, " then you'll ask the Knight to spare my life, and he'll say all right, if I solemnly promise never to eat any more children, and I'll promise–why shouldn't I?–and then we'll all go home to tea."

22

"Well, it's worth trying anyway," said Tony.
"Wait here till I come back."

It was some time before Tony returned from his
visit to the Knight, but when he did he was smiling
all over his face.

"It's all right!" he called out as soon as he saw

the dragon. "He'll do it! He said would you promise *cross your heart* to let him win and I said, on the heart of a dragon, you would. And the fight's to be tomorrow, in Father's top field, at three o'clock."

"Good," said Albert calmly. "I'll be there, and I'll give them a show worth watching. Trust me!"

Next afternoon the top field was crowded with people, all in their best clothes and all with baskets of food. Promptly at three o'clock the Knight rode grandly into the middle of the field on his big black horse and everyone cheered. Next moment a loud roaring was heard, rather like an express train coming out of a tunnel, and Albert burst through the crowd lashing his tail, rippling his scales, and breathing fire and smoke through his nostrils. The crowd drew back rather nervously. They had never seen their tame old dragon look like that before, and although they knew perfectly well that he never ate children or did any harm at all, just for a moment they couldn't help wondering. But the Knight sat firm as a rock in his saddle, and then, raising his lance, he charged full tilt at Albert!

What a battle that was! No one who was there ever forgot it, and even Tony, who knew perfectly well how it was to end, got so excited that he jumped up and down and shouted himself hoarse.

24

"Come on Dragon! Come on our side! Up and at him, Albert!" he cried. Albert, hearing him, re-doubled his efforts and blew such clouds of smoke

out of his nostrils that for a time the spectators could see nothing of the battle at all.

"Less smoke, Albert!" yelled Tony, and the dragon paused long enough in the fight to wave a reassuring claw in his direction.

And then a dreadful thing happened. You see, no one had thought of explaining to the Knight's *horse* that the whole fight was a put up job, so naturally he imagined his master was out to kill Albert, and he watched his opportunity and suddenly gave the dragon a tremendous kick in the ribs!

Albert was furious! The kick didn't hurt, his scales were too thick for that, being like metal plating, but it did tickle and he had particularly said he wasn't to be tickled. He couldn't help laughing because—well—you always do laugh when you're tickled, don't you? But he was angry too, so his laugh came out in short, furious *ha has* and sounded very fierce indeed. In fact it frightened the horse so

26

much that he reared up on his hind legs, turned round and round, nearly throwing the Knight out of the saddle, and then dropping to the ground again, dashed right out of the field and away until both horse and rider disappeared from sight over the brow of the hill!

For a moment everyone was so astonished they just stood silently, staring after the bolting horse. Albert lay in the middle of the field, still wriggling and giggling from being tickled. Tony stood with his mouth open, and just gaped. And then everyone began to laugh. How they laughed! It was a good thing the Knight was no longer there to hear them because it would have made his ears burn. Then they began to cheer Albert and tell each other they always knew their dear old dragon would win, and who *was* this Knight anyway, to come butting in and trying to save them from their own dragon! They all went home in a very good humour, swearing they hadn't had such a good day out for years!

But Albert felt a bit uncomfortable. He wondered what Tony was thinking, because after all, the bargain had been that the Knight should be allowed to win, and he very definitely hadn't. Albert looked sideways at Tony, and blew out a little steam in an apologetic way. But Tony was laughing too.

" Oh Albert! " he managed to get out between giggles. " If you could have seen your face, when the horse tickled you! I thought you were going to burst, I really did! Oh dear, I've got a pain in my middle from laughing so much!"

Albert shot him a glance. He tidied himself up, rippled his scales back into place so that they changed from green to blue, puffed a little smoke out of his nose, shook his head, lashed his tail and then said just one word.

"Horses!" said Albert, and led the way down the hill to his cave.

Albert breaks the record

Albert the dragon spent a good deal of his time on a flat slab of rock outside the cave where he lived. On fine days he dozed in the sun, and on wet days he took advantage of the rain by having a good bath. On the day Tony came up the path to visit his friend, Albert had had a nice wash in a sharp shower of rain and was now drying himself by shaking like a great dog, and flapping his short, stumpy wings vigorously in the air.

Tony stopped short, amazed.

"Albert," he exclaimed, "all this time I've known you, and you never told me you had wings!"

"Oh, didn't I mention it?" enquired Albert carelessly. "I thought you knew. Of course they don't show at all when they're folded away. But they're rather nice, don't you think?" he said modestly, spreading the wings wide, to let Tony see their strength, and the beauty of the blue and green scales shimmering in the sunlight.

29

"Nice? I should think they are!" said Tony enviously. "But Albert, if you've got wings, why on earth don't you fly?"

"Fly?" said Albert. "Oh, I couldn't do that, my dear chap. Dragons don't fly."

"How d'you know they don't?" said Tony coming closer and feeling the wings admiringly. "You're such an old stick-in-the-mud, Albert, you never go anywhere or mix with other dragons, you don't really know what they're up to."

"There's something in what you say," agreed Albert thoughtfully.

"I bet you anything you like," said Tony, "that dragons are flying all over the place. Stands to reason. If you've got wings, you're meant to fly. Only wish I had them. Flying must be glorious."

"You think so?" enquired Albert doubtfully.

"Yes, I do. And think of the time you'd save. Whenever you wanted to go down to the beach to eat seaweed, you'd just flap there and back in no time instead of having to plod all the way down and climb all the way back. And you're not very quick on your legs, you know you're not, Albert."

"I'm quick enough for my needs," said Albert a little huffily. "But all the same, I don't mind having a try at this flying business. Er–how do you think I should start?"

"Can't you just take off?"

"I doubt it. I don't feel as if I could. I'm sure one must have confidence first, like swimming, you know. And suppose I get up and then fall? I should hurt myself awfully on this rocky ground."

"I know!" exclaimed Tony. "Jump off the cliffs! Then if you do fall you'll only fall into the sea."

"It's an idea," said Albert slowly. "And yet—well—would *you* like to jump off the cliffs, Tony?"

"If I had wings like yours I'd love it. Look here, Albert, you're not *scared*, are you?"

"*Scared?* My dear fellow, I think you must be joking," said Albert stiffly, and Tony said quickly:

"Sorry, of course you aren't. Well then come on. I just can't wait to see you sailing off grandly into the air."

When they arrived at the cliff top Albert crawled to the edge and looked at the sea. It seemed a very long way down. Then he looked up at the air, unfolded his wings, flapped them once or twice and paused.

"Go on," said Tony impatiently, "what are you waiting for?"

"Tony," said the dragon, and try as he would he couldn't keep his voice quite steady, "Tony, just give me a little shove, will you, like a good chap?"

"Certainly," said Tony, and he got behind the dragon and pushed with all his strength.

"Go on, push," said Albert. "Don't be afraid of hurting me."

"I *am* pushing," said Tony crossly, mopping his forehead. "I can't move you, you're far too heavy. Why don't you jump?"

The dragon closed his eyes. "I'll count three," he thought to himself. "No I won't, I'll count ten, and then I'll jump."

"One, two, three," he counted. "After all, if I fall I'll only get wet–four, five, six, seven–but how Tony will laugh–eight, nine, TEN!" And he jumped!

The next moment he found himself flying, with strong, steady wing beats, just over the surface of the sea.

"This is glorious!" he thought. "What a fool I've been never to try it before! All these years I've crawled about practically on my tummy owing to my legs being so short, and all the time I might have been flying like this. Good old Tony! What a brain that boy's got!" And he turned and flew back to the cliff, circling round Tony's head and waving a claw gaily as he passed. He tried one or two more little flights out to sea and then landed carefully on the short turf of the cliff top.

"That was jolly good, Albert!" cried Tony. "Oh, you are lucky. I wish I could fly! I say, Albert, couldn't I ride on your back?"

AD—C

" Well, I suppose it would be possible," said Albert doubtfully. "Don't think I'm making difficulties, old boy, but it's a bit of a responsibility for me. I mean, suppose you slipped or anything? I'd never hear the last of it from your mother."

" I wouldn't slip," said Tony scornfully. " I'll tell you what though, I might bring a rope from home and put it round your neck, just to hold on to. What do you think? "

"Well," said Albert, " I suppose you *could*. But a rope? I don't much like the idea of that. You couldn't manage a silken cord, I suppose? I feel somehow it would be more–how shall I put it–more suitable for me. What do you think? "

" I don't think there are any silken cords in our farmhouse," said Tony. " What I had in mind was Mother's clothes line, if I can pinch it when she's not looking. Come on, Albert–be a sport! "

" Oh, very well. It doesn't matter. Just an idea I had. I thought a golden, or perhaps a scarlet cord against my green scales would look rather smart, but forget it, Tony, forget it. Run and get your mother's –er–clothes line and we'll be off. A quick circuit round Cornwall, I think, and then perhaps a flap over to the Scilly Isles? That suit you? "

" Wonderful! " said Tony, and he dashed off to fetch the rope.

An hour later they were on their way. The dragon, now quite at home in the air, made a wide circle round the whole county and they both looked down with the greatest interest on towns and villages they had never seen before. Then Albert turned in the direction of Land's End, and soon they were beating their way strongly over the open sea.

Half-way across to the islands Tony suddenly bent forward and shouted in the dragon's ear:

"I say, Albert! I've had a wonderful idea! Why shouldn't you be the first dragon to fly the Atlantic?"

Albert was so startled he gave a great leap in the air and Tony had to cling to the rope with both hands to keep his seat.

"Hey!" Tony yelled. "Stop that! You nearly bounced me off. Don't you like the idea?"

Albert thought for a moment, flying steadily on towards the Scilly Isles, now just coming into view.

"What for?" he said at last.

"What *for?* Well, for–for–the adventure and to make you the most famous dragon in England."

"It's a long way," said Albert, "and I shouldn't know a soul on the other side when I got there."

"You soon would!" shouted Tony. "You'd be made a tremendous fuss of. You'd be a terribly grand sort of person, Albert. People who do things for the first time always are."

35

Albert suddenly made up his mind. He was tired of being called a stick-in-the-mud, and it was quite true what Tony said, that he never went anywhere or did anything. Also he had a suspicion that Tony thought him just a little bit of a coward, although Tony was too much of a friend to show it, and he couldn't bear that.

"All right," he said. "I will. I'll fly there and back, starting tomorrow." And although his heart sank at the thought, he began to feel most awfully brave and adventurous.

"Good for you!" cried Tony. "I'll tell everyone, and they'll all come to see you off and wish you luck, and–good gracious! Just look over there!"

Albert looked where his rider was pointing and gasped with surprise. They were now very close to the Scilly Isles, and there, flying over the islands, were dozens and dozens of other dragons! The air was full of their huge bodies and beating wings, and the sun, glinting on their blue and green and orange scales sent out flashes of bright light which made Tony and Albert blink. As they drew nearer they could see that all the dragons were circling round one special dragon, a huge chap who was lying on the ground apparently resting, and behind him was a great banner with something written on it. Tony spelt it out.

36

" Oh *Albert!* " he cried in dismay. " Look what it says on that banner! "

Now Albert couldn't read, but he wouldn't have let Tony know this for all the world, so he flew lower, circled round the banner and said :

" Hum, very odd! What do you make it out to be, Tony? I wonder if we both think the same thing? "

" Well, it's plain enough, isn't it? " said Tony. " Only too plain, worse luck. *Welcome Home to Percival. The First Dragon to fly the Atlantic both ways*. That's what it says, and I think it's hateful! " And poor Tony turned away his head to hide his tears of disappointment.

But Albert suddenly felt quite light-hearted. If someone else had done it first, that let him out, and he hadn't wanted to fly the Atlantic in the least. He felt a nice, warm feeling of gratitude to the unknown Percival, whom he now admitted to be a very fine figure of a dragon indeed.

" Never mind, old fellow," he said comfortingly to Tony. " We can't all be first, you know, and I'm such an old stick-in-the-mud I might never have got there at all and then think how silly I should have looked. You must have to be awfully strong for these trans-Atlantic flights and I expect this Percival chap trained on meat of–er–some kind, and I couldn't do that, because you know I only eat grass. Cheer up, Tony, do, it's really all for the best."

37

"It's all very well . . ." Tony was beginning in a doleful voice, when something quite unexpected happened. A small, bright green dragon with a bustling, important manner flew up to them and shouted:

"I say! you there! "

"Speaking to me? " enquired Albert, and he blew a little smoke, rather shyly, through his nose.

"I should jolly well think I am! " exclaimed the bright green dragon flying alongside excitedly. "I simply couldn't believe my eyes when I saw you. Is that actually a human being you're carrying on your back? "

"A human? " asked Albert, puzzled. "It's Tony, if that's what you mean. He's a great friend of mine. I suppose you'd call him human. Why do you ask? "

"My dear chap! " exclaimed the small dragon. "You don't seem to realize how extraordinary it is! You behave as if it were a perfectly ordinary thing. Why, you must be, in fact I'm sure you *are*, the very first dragon ever to carry a human on his back! It's a new record! You'll be famous! This is much more exciting than Percival's dull old trip over the Atlantic and back! This has–well–*human* interest! Come along, you must land. Everyone will want to meet you! "

"Oh no," said Albert hastily, "I don't think I

will, if you don't mind awfully. I'm rather a shy sort of chap–"

"Nonsense!" cried the bright green dragon. "I won't take no for an answer! We're just going to have a feast to celebrate Percival's record, so you

must come too, and sit at the other end of the table. Percival won't like it, but who cares? He wants taking down a peg anyway. If ever a dragon suffered from a swelled head, he does! Come on now, this way down! "

He led the way to a landing place right in the middle of the crowd of dragons, and explained to them excitedly all about Albert and the new record he had established. They were the friendliest crowd, and Albert and Tony soon felt quite at ease. A long table was brought out and loaded with all kinds of delicious food, and Albert was made to sit at one end under a new banner hastily painted by an elderly dragon with a blue head. It read WELCOME TO ALBERT! THE FIRST DRAGON TO FLY WITH A HUMAN PASSENGER!

The only person who didn't look happy was Percival, who sulked under his banner at the other end of the table. Albert couldn't help feeling sorry about this because he knew in his heart of hearts that Percival had done something much bigger and more important than he had, and so presently he got up and slipped round the table and said:

"Percival, old chap, I've simply got to shake you by the claw, I think you're *wonderful!*"

Percival hesitated a moment, and then his scowl turned to a smile as he saw the real admiration in

Albert's face. He gave a modest little laugh and said:

"Oh, it was nothing really, just a little flap," and he took Albert's claw and shook it heartily!

When Albert and Tony finally got back home it was nearly bed-time and they were both tired.

"Well, goodnight, Albert," said Tony yawning. "I'm glad you beat the record at something, even if you didn't fly the Atlantic. I bet you could have though, if you'd wanted to."

"I daresay," said Albert carelessly, "but I never was the chap to push myself forward."

He went sleepily into the cave and flopped down. His eyes shut. Then they opened again.

"I should have been terrified!" he whispered to himself, and fell thankfully asleep.

Albert and the Feather Bed

One morning in early Spring, when the birds were nesting and the lambs were crying and calling in the fields, Albert the dragon came out of his cave and lay down in the warm sunlight. He blinked his eyes happily and stretched all his huge, scaly body in the pleasant warmth, and was just beginning to feel delightfully drowsy when he was roused by the sound of footsteps coming up the steep path towards him.

"I hope that's Tony," he thought to himself. "If it is I'll suggest that we take our lunch out and have a picnic." But as the footsteps drew nearer, Albert knew they did not belong to Tony, they were too slow, for one thing, and too heavy, for another. Albert sat up rather anxiously. He didn't like strangers coming to his cave. The footsteps were quite close now, and the next second he saw the burly form of the village postman coming round the corner. Albert was astonished! The postman had never come near his cave before, in fact the dragon had never had a letter in his life!

42

The postman stopped when he saw Albert, and stood puffing and blowing and looking just a little bit anxious. He knew of course that Albert was no ordinary dragon, that he was kind and good and never, never ate anything except grass and seaweed, and certainly never postmen, who would be very tough anyway, from walking so much. But all the same, he thought Albert looked very big and very scaly, and surely that *was* smoke coming out of his nose? So he stopped at a safe distance and held out a letter at arm's length.

"Name of Albert?" he enquired, although he knew perfectly well who Albert was.

"That's right," said Albert. "Is that letter for me?"

The postman said it was, and Albert took it carefully in one claw and looked at it with the greatest interest.

"Aren't you going to open it and read it?" enquired the postman.

"Er–no, not just now," said Albert. He wasn't going to let the postman know he couldn't read.

"Go on," said the postman. "It might be something important. I can take an answer for you, if you like."

Albert got rather cross, and when he got cross he got hot, and that made more smoke and even small flames come out of his nose.

" Now look here, postman," he said. " Is this your letter or mine? "

"Yours," said the postman, looking at the smoke and flames and beginning to back down the steep path. "Yours, old man, not a doubt of that."

" Then leave me to do what I think best with it," said Albert sternly. " Oh, and by the way, postman, if you should see Tony on your way down, ask him to step up here at his earliest convenience, would you? "

The postman promised he would, and Albert sat down on his rock again and looked at the letter carefully all over, but he simply could not guess who had written it or what it could be about. He shook it and held it up to the light, he even opened the envelope and took the sheet of paper out, but not being able to read he was no wiser than before.

"Who *can* be writing to me? " he thought. " It's not my birthday, so it can't be anyone saying ' many happy returns ', and it's not a bill because I don't owe any money. I don't know what it can be."

At that moment, to his great relief, he heard Tony hurrying up the path. He got up and, still holding the letter, went to meet him.

" Hullo Albert," said Tony. " Puff, it's quite hot. What's this I hear about you getting a letter? "

"A letter? " said Albert casually. He wasn't going

to let anyone know how excited he felt. " A *letter?*
Oh yes, of course. I did get one this morning. Now
what did I do with it? Oh yes, here it is in my claw.
Would you like to read it, Tony? "

" I will if you like," said Tony. " Who's it from? "

" You'll see when you read it," said Albert cun-
ningly.

Tony took the letter and read it, but instead of
reading it aloud, as Albert had planned he should
do, he read it to himself. Albert nearly died of
curiosity. When Tony had finished reading, he
folded the letter, put it back in its envelope and
handed it to Albert.

" Well? " said Albert, " what do you think of
that? "

" Not much," said Tony. " It sounds as if she
would be the most awful bore."

This nearly drove Albert wild, but he still
wouldn't admit that he didn't know what the letter
said.

" Why a bore? " he enquired carefully, and Tony
said :

" Well, visitors *are* a bore, aren't they? You have
to wear tidy clothes—not you, I don't mean, but me—
and ask them what *they* want to play and all that sort
of thing."

" *Visitors?* " thought Albert to himself. " Visitors
for me? Who can they be? " Aloud he said :

45

"Do they say when they're coming? I–er–can't quite remember."

"Tomorrow, isn't it?" said Tony. "And it isn't them, it's her."

"*Her?*" said Albert. "Tony, are you sure?"

"Well, you ought to know," said Tony. "After all it's your aunt, not mine."

At that Albert had to give in. Aunts were a serious matter, and if the letter was from an aunt, the sooner he knew exactly what it said, the better.

"Tony, old boy," he said in a low voice. "Don't laugh please, but well, to tell the truth I–I–don't know what's in that letter. Tony, the fact is, I can't read!"

Now Tony was a real little gentleman. Some small boys might have jeered at a dragon who couldn't read, but not Tony! All *he* did was to hold out his hand for the letter and say, in the kindest manner:

"Lots of people can't read, old chap. There's nothing in that. I'll soon tell you what it says." And he read aloud:

> The Cave
> St Anthony in Roseland
> Cornwall

My dear Nephew Albert,

I have had a bad cold and need a change of air, so I

shall come and spend a week with you, arriving tomorrow. Please see that the bed is *well aired*

–"She underlined that three times," said Tony.

–and get in plenty of mussels as I am on a fish diet. Expect me about tea time.

Your affectionate aunt,
Emmeline Dragon

"Oh dear, oh dear, oh dear!" exclaimed Albert when Tony had finished reading. "You were perfectly right, Tony, it *is* a bore! And Tony, what does she mean about airing the bed? I haven't *got* a bed. I just sleep on the floor."

"Then air the floor," said Tony with a giggle.

"Oh, if you're going to be silly–" said Albert huffily.

"I'm sorry, Albert," said Tony, "but it *is* rather funny, you know. You with an aunt! But I'll tell you what I'll do. I'll ask my mother to lend you her second best feather bed!"

"Oh Tony, will you *really?*" said Albert with great relief. "I should think that would be just the thing for Aunt Emmeline! Oh, my goodness, I really shall have to tidy up a bit. I haven't had a real, good clean-up since–since–well, I don't think I've *ever* had a real good clean-up now I come to think of it."

"Then you'd better make a start," suggested Tony. "But first come down to the farm with me and we'll fetch the bed."

"But are you sure your mother will lend it to me?" asked Albert.

"Oh yes, I'm sure she will," Tony said. "But anyway, I've just remembered she's gone to town to-day, so we'll take it first and ask afterwards. Come on!"

Getting the feather bed up the steep, stony path to the cave was hard work, and it really wasn't Albert's fault that he got so hot he burnt a small hole in the corner of the bed. It was a pity though, as Tony pointed out, because the feathers simply poured through the hole and left a trail all the way up the path.

"They'll think–the fox–has carried off–one of our geese," panted Tony, red in the face with exertion as he toiled up the hill. " Do–keep going, Albert –when you stop–like that–the bed–pushes me back-

ward–and I'm nearly smothered. Are we nearly there? "

They reached the cave at last and arranged the feather bed tidily in one corner and covered it over with Albert's best patchwork quilt. Then they swept up the feathers as best they could, threw out a lot of old rubbish which lay about on the floor, dusted around with Tony's hankie and straightened the sampler which had been worked by Albert's mother and which read:

> Do the job that's nearest
> Though 'tis dull at whiles,
> Helping when you meet them
> Lame dragons over stiles.

When they had finished they both thought the cave looked splendid and quite worthy of any aunt.

" Now," said Albert, " all I have to do is go down to the beach and gather a good supply of mussels. Coming, Tony? "

Tony was just about to reply when he stopped short and they both listened intently. Someone was coming slowly up the path and talking to themselves as they came!

" Oh, my goodness, good gracious! " they heard a voice say. " Oh, my dearie dear! Can't go out a minute but that pesky fox do come and steal my geese. But I'll give 'im geese! Just let 'im wait till I catch up with 'im. Feathers, feathers, all the way! Did you ever see the like of that?"

"Albert!" said Tony. "It's Mother! And, oh dear, she does sound cross!"

They peeped round the corner of the cave, and there, sure enough, was Tony's stout mother, toiling up the path, very red in the face.

"Tony!" whispered Albert. "I don't feel very happy about having borrowed the bed without asking."

"Neither do I!" said Tony. "Hush! Keep quiet! Here she is!"

They cowered back in the shadow of the cave, but the next second Tony's mother looked in and saw them.

"Ha!" she said. "Tony, my boy, have you seen the fox? He's took one of my geese I do believe, for there's a trail of feathers from here right down to the farmyard."

She came a little further, and now she saw the bed with Albert hovering anxiously before it.

"My gracious goodness!" she said, "My second best feather bed! My dear life, don't tell me the fox took it, for I'll never believe it!"

"It wasn't the fox," said Albert in a trembling voice, "it was—me."

Oh, how angry Tony's mother was! Albert tried to explain about his aunt but she wouldn't listen to a word! And when she whisked off the patchwork quilt and saw the great burnt hole with feathers still coming out, well, you could have heard her from there all the way to the next town! Nothing would suit her but Albert and Tony must pick up the bed again and carry it straight back to the farm, while she walked alongside holding the burnt edges of the hole together as best she could to keep the feathers in!

Back in the cave later, Albert and Tony sat down side by side in the deepest gloom. Albert was in despair at the thought of having to face his Aunt Emmeline without a bed, to say nothing of a well-aired bed, and Tony was miserable because he had got Albert into trouble. They were so wretched that they didn't even hear the postman until he arrived before them and held out *another* letter to Albert!

" Oh Tony! " said poor Albert when the postman had gone. " This is more than I can bear! Suppose—suppose it should be from *another* aunt! "

" Have you got another one? " asked Tony sensibly.

" Not that I know of," said Albert, " but it's hard to be quite sure."

Tony opened the letter, glanced quickly at it and then said :

" Cheer up, Albert! It's all right. Listen! " And he read :

52

The Cave
St Anthony in Roseland
Cornwall

Dear Nephew Albert,
Have you got a feather bed? If not, I shan't come.
Your affectionate aunt,
Emmeline Dragon

"Oh Tony!" exclaimed Albert. "Isn't it wonderful how things turn out for the best! If your mother hadn't come up here and been so cross and taken the bed away I couldn't have truthfully said I hadn't got one, and then Aunt Emmeline would have come for sure! Quick, Tony, write a letter for me and I'll dash down to send it off!"

"O.K.," said Tony. "What shall I say?"

Albert thought very deeply for several minutes, then he said:

"Write this, Tony,

Dear Aunt Emmeline,
No.
Your affectionate nephew,
Albert"

Albert builds a house

One Spring day when the primroses were in bloom and the lambs in the fields, Albert the dragon came out of his cave and looked all round with great pleasure.

" Glorious day! " said Albert to himself. " Good to be alive! "

He sniffed the air, then flapped his short, stumpy wings and drew in deep breaths as he did so.

" One–two–one–two! " counted Albert. " Ah, that's better. I've been stuffed up in that cave for too long. I must get out more. It will be good for my health! "

He said the last words aloud, and then jumped violently as a voice behind him said:

" What's the matter with your health, Albert? "

" Oh, how you startled me! " exclaimed Albert, leaping round with a claw on his heart. " It's you, is it, Tony? I wish you wouldn't creep up on me like that! "

54

" I didn't creep! " said Tony indignantly. " I clattered my feet like anything, only you were so busy talking to yourself you didn't hear me. Are you ill? "

" Of course I'm not ill," said Albert with dignity. " I enjoy excellent health, thank you. Why do you ask? "

" Well, you were talking to yourself about something being good for you," argued Tony.

" You are quite right," said Albert generously. " I was. I was saying I must get out into the fresh air more often. I spend too much time in that stuffy old cave."

" I've always said so," said Tony. " But *you* always say you like it."

" I have been mistaken," admitted Albert. " It takes a lovely, fresh Spring day like this to show me how mistaken I have been. Now, my dear boy, you have an excellent brain, what do you think I should do? "

" About what? " asked Tony.

"Tony, my friend," said Albert reproachfully, "are you trying to make me cross? Because if so," he went on, speaking rather quickly and puffing a little smoke out of his nostrils, "if so, you are succeeding!"

"Sorry," said Tony. "I didn't mean to upset you, Albert. You mean, what do I think you ought to do about getting more fresh air? Is that it?"

"Exactly," said Albert, and he looked expectantly at Tony, who thought hard.

"I wish I could think like that," said Albert admiringly. "But when I really try to think my brain goes all funny and I feel queer."

"What sort of queer?" asked Tony with interest.

"Dizzy," said Albert. "Have you thought yet?"

"As a matter of fact I have," said Tony. "It's obvious what you ought to do. If your cave is stuffy –and I'm sure it is, right underground like that–you must build a house."

"A house!" exclaimed Albert. "Tony, my boy, what a magnificent idea! Of course! A house! I could call it Dragon Castle!"

"You can't call it a castle unless it *is* a castle," argued Tony. "And a proper castle would be an awful bore to build. You'd have to carry masses of rocks up from the seashore. Awfully hard work it would be."

"Not a castle then," said Albert quickly. "After

all, it would be a bit too grand for the likes of me. A manor house then! Dragon Manor!"

Tony shook his head. "If you have a manor then you'll be Lord of the Manor, and you'll have to look after everyone who lives on your land and always have food ready for them if they come to the kitchen door and ask for it."

"I couldn't do that," Albert admitted. "For one thing they wouldn't like my sort of food–grass and small trees and seaweed. They'd want bread, and beef."

"Of course they would!" Tony agreed. "Better not have a manor then."

Albert thought hard, and it was easy to see that it really did make him dizzy. He went quite pale, and closed his eyes and swayed from side to side.

"Here! hold up!" exclaimed Tony. "You nearly squashed me against that rock. Do look out!"

"Sorry," said Albert. "But I have thought of something! Dragon Farm!"

"Oh, don't be silly," said Tony wearily. "How can you have a farm without animals, and what animals do you think would come and work for a dragon? They'd be afraid of you!"

"Then what do you suggest, Tony?" asked Albert humbly.

"I suggest a small hut of wood and straw in my father's top field," said Tony briskly. "Nothing

57

grand. No castles or manors or farms. Just a nice, comfortable hut, with plenty of big windows to let in the fresh air."

"What a brain you've got!" said Albert admiringly. "I should never have thought of that in a thousand years. Of course! Just a hut, humble, and yet artistic. I could call it 'The Nest'."

"Well, I suppose you could," admitted Tony. "But if you don't mind my saying so, Albert, it sounds jolly silly. Whoever heard of a dragon's nest?"

Albert sighed.

"All right," he said. "What would you call it, Tony?"

"I should call it Number One, Top Field," said Tony. "That's sensible, that is, and people will know exactly where you are."

"They'd know anyway," objected Albert. "I mean to say, a hut large enough to take me isn't going to be so very small. People are bound to see it as soon as they come into the field. And isn't it rather silly to say 'Number One' when there aren't any others?"

"How you do argue," said Tony rather crossly. "All right then, call it 'Albert Villa'."

"Now I like that!" said Albert. "Yes, I like that very much. 'Albert Villa'! It has style, don't you think?"

"I think it's loony," said Tony, "but have it your own way. The important thing is to build it, not name it. You seem to have forgotten that."

"I've been turning it over in my mind all the time," said Albert reproachfully. "I'm not as silly as you think I am, Tony. Wood and straw you said, didn't you? Where should I get them?"

"I can get you the straw out of Dad's barn," said Tony. "That's for the roof, you know. The wood you'll have to get yourself. If you go down to the beach you'll find plenty of driftwood. Sometimes you can find quite big planks."

"What! Carry it all the way from the beach to your father's top field?" exclaimed Albert in dismay. "It would be almost as bad as carrying up rocks for a castle!"

"Of course it wouldn't," said Tony. "Nothing like. I'll tell you what, Albert, if I were to tie the wood on to your back you could *fly* it up!"

"I suppose I could," said Albert thoughtfully. "That would save my poor old legs, wouldn't it?"

"What's the matter with your legs?" asked Tony.

"Nothing," said Albert. "Nothing, except that they are rather short, and they ache terribly going uphill!" He tried to look pathetic so that Tony would be sorry for him, but Tony only laughed and said:

"You are in a complaining sort of mood today!

59

I'll tell you this, Albert. I wouldn't bother a bit about my legs if I had wings like yours. You're jolly lucky, and you don't fly half enough."

"I can't rid myself of a dreadful fear that I might *drop*," Albert confessed. "I know it's silly, but there it is."

"You won't drop," said Tony. "Birds don't, unless someone shoots them down, so why should dragons?"

Albert started nervously.

"I never thought of shooting!" he said. "Oh, Tony . . ."

"Do you really suppose," said Tony, speaking very slowly and patiently, "that anyone could shoot you through those scales of yours? Nothing could possibly go through. Now, come on, Albert, let's start at once."

They went down the steep path one behind the other, because it was so narrow, stopping at Tony's house on the way to borrow a rope. When they got to the beach, there, sure enough, were lots of planks and other bits of wood, lying on the sand, or bobbing about in the little waves which lapped the shore. Tony and Albert set to work busily and soon had a big pile of wood, heaped up and ready to be taken to the field far above.

"Now then, Albert," said Tony, "I've got to tie this pile on your back with the rope. Lie down and make yourself as flat as possible so that I can fix it on."

Albert lay down and made himself as flat as he could, but this wasn't very flat because of the spiny ridge which all dragons have down the middle of their backs.

"Bother!" said Tony as the wood fell off for the

tenth time. " This isn't going to work, Albert. Now what are we going to do? It isn't funny! " he added crossly to a line of seagulls who were perched on a nearby rock, laughing their heads off.

" Be off with you! " said Albert sharply, and he puffed smoke out of his nostrils at the seagulls, who all rose up into the air with frightened squawks.

" I'll tell you what we'd better do," said Tony suddenly. " We'd better tie the wood into a bundle and then tie the other end of the rope to your tail. Then you can fly off and the wood will dangle below. You'll have to fly quite high so as not to hit anyone on the ground. Think you can do it, Albert? "

" I suppose so," grumbled Albert. " But a nice figure of fun I shall look, I must say! "

" Now see here! " demanded Tony. " Do you want a house or don't you? You do? Then don't make so many difficulties or we shall never get it built. There! Now I've tied all this lot of wood to-gether. Twice round your tail, Albert, and then off you go! "

" Are you coming too? " asked Albert. " I'll give you a lift if you like."

Tony shook his head.

" I'll stay here and collect more wood," he said. " You can untie the rope when you get there, can't you? Then go on! "

Albert rose slowly into the air with a great flapping of wings and sailed slowly and majestically upwards, the wood dangling below, until he disappeared from sight over the top of the cliffs. Tony went on collecting wood, and presently Albert returned, slightly out of breath, and alighted at his side.

"You needn't have tied that knot so tight," he complained. "I've strained my back twisting round to get it untied from my tail! But I've chosen a lovely spot for the Castle–er–*hut*–Tony! Under the rowan tree and in the shelter of the hedge. It has a glorious view out to sea. I know I'm going to love living up there! It was a wonderful idea of yours, Tony, my friend. Thank you a thousand times!"

"You're welcome," said Tony. "And now, if you'd stop talking so much and do some work. . . ."

"Very sorry, I'm sure!" said Albert huffily and he began to get a little bit hot because he was annoyed with the way Tony spoke to him. The smoke came out of his nostrils in little puffs and his beautiful bluey-green scales began to turn red with heat.

"Here, steady on!" said Tony. "You're making me feel hot and that plank you're holding is beginning to scorch. Sorry if I said anything to upset you, old boy."

"It's nothing," said Albert. "I'm much too touchy. I know I am; it's my greatest fault. I'll just have a little paddle to cool myself down."

63

He waded into the water, which sizzled as it washed against his legs.

"I was heated!" said Albert. "I mustn't do that again. Is the next load ready? Then off we go!"

By sun-down Tony and Albert, working very hard, had collected enough wood in Tony's father's top field to build the hut, and they went to bed well satisfied with their day's work. As Albert stretched himself out in his cave that night he thought drowsily:

"Last night in this stuffy old cave! Tomorrow night I shall be sleeping in my beautiful, airy hut, with the soft night breeze blowing on my face, and the branches of the rowan tree rustling sleepily over-head and the stars peeping in at my window!"

He was up at dawn, and was hard at work on the walls of the hut by the time Tony arrived with a load of straw for the roof.

"My word!" said Tony, putting down the straw with a sigh of relief and fanning himself with his hat. "You have got on, Albert! You'll be able to sleep in here tonight."

"That's what I thought," said Albert. "Oh, Tony, it is going to be fun! How I could ever have lived in that dark old cave when there was all this beautiful fresh air up above I just can't think. How-ever, better late than never! Would you like to come and sleep here too? I think there would be room, if we squeezed up a bit tightish."

"No, thanks," said Tony, looking at the sharp spines on Albert's back. "I think I like my own room best."

"Please yourself," said Albert amiably. "If you change your mind you have only to say so. Now, my boy, I think we are ready to put on the roof."

They thatched the roof with straw, in exactly the same way that Tony had seen his father thatch the barn roof, and when they had finished the hut really looked very nice. Albert was so excited about it he kept darting in and out and waving at Tony, first through one window and then through the other. Then he made Tony knock on the door, and pretended he didn't know who it was and was tremendously surprised when he opened it and found Tony on the doorstep. They were having lots of fun when suddenly a sneering voice said:

"What's that thing supposed to be? A beehive?"

Albert and Tony both turned round in surprise and saw an old, grey donkey looking at them over the hedge.

"Of course it's not a beehive!" cried Albert indignantly. "I should think anyone could see it was a hut! It's called 'Albert Villa'."

"'Albert Villa'!" repeated the donkey, and he

brayed with laughter. It was a horrid sound and both Tony and Albert felt themselves getting hot with anger. With Tony that didn't matter, but with Albert–!

"Look out!" yelled Tony. "Albert! Cool down! You'll set the hut on fire!"

"Set the beehive on fire, you mean!" giggled the donkey, and that made poor Albert, who really had been trying to control his temper, simply boil with rage! His scales glowed orange and red with heat and not only smoke but flames shot out of his nose! The hut blazed up like a bonfire on Guy Fawkes night and Tony and Albert had to run for their lives. They ran to the end of the field, farthest away from the donkey, who was laughing his silly head off on the other side of the hedge.

But Albert was in tears. His glowing scales faded to pale green again and the tears simply poured down his face.

"Oh, Albert!" cried Tony. "Don't be sorrowful! Please don't! We'll build another hut tomorrow–a better hut. I'll–I'll make Dad sell that beastly donkey in the market! Please, Albert, don't cry any more."

Albert managed a very wan smile.

"Don't do that," he said. "The poor old chap didn't mean any harm. Perhaps he thought it really *was* a beehive. I think I'll go home now, Tony, if you

66

don't mind. I've got a bit of a headache. See you to-morrow, and thanks for all your help."

He went down the steep path till he reached the entrance to his cave, then stopped and looked in. The cave really looked very snug. A bright fire blazed on the hearth and the flames were reflected in all his little bits of copper and brass. Albert went slowly in and sat down in his favourite chair by the fire. A chilly little wind had sprung up outside and as he listened, the first drops of rain pattered on the flat stone at the entrance to the cave.

"Fresh air be–*bothered!*" said Albert contentedly.

Albert and the Sea Serpent

It was on a hot, sunshiny day that Albert the dragon first saw the sea serpent. He was down on the beach at Tregunna Cove with his friend Tony when they both saw something queer at the same moment.

"What's that?" they both said together. Tony shaded his eyes with his hand and stared out to sea.

"It's a school of porpoises," he said. "Leaping out of the water. That's what it is."

Albert shaded *his* eyes with a claw.

"Well, you may be right, Tony, I'm not saying you aren't," he said. "But I don't think that's porpoises."

"Well, what is it then?" said Tony.

"I don't know, but I'm going to find out. You stay here, my boy, and I'll just fly round and try and spot what it is."

"Take me with you," urged Tony, but Albert said: "No. Definitely no. Suppose you fell off and that thing, whatever it is, was dangerous? No, you stay here, and I'll come straight back and tell you what it is."

"Here, wait a minute!" said Tony. "Don't go yet. I believe it's coming in to land."

The thing they were watching was certainly very queer. It looked rather like a lot of old car wheels floating upright half out of the water, one behind the other, but there were no cars in those days so of course it couldn't be that.

The car wheel things came gliding through the water at a great rate, and as they approached the land the watchers could see that the loops were black and shiny and that the front one was rearing up on end and seemed to have a face.

Tony and Albert stood amazed. They had never seen anything like this before in all their lives, and the thought did just cross their minds that it might be wiser to scramble up the cliff path as quickly as possible and look down at the thing safely from above. They weren't *afraid*, they only wanted to behave sensibly.

Just as they turned to go, a voice hailed them from the sea.

"Hi!" said the voice, "don't go!"

They stopped, and looked round.

"Good gracious!" exclaimed Albert. "I know what that is! It's a sea serpent!"

" Of course I am," said the voice, " though I must say it's not very polite to call me ' it '. My name, if it interests you, is Sidney."

Albert pulled himself together and remembered his manners.

" Terribly sorry, old chap," he said, " you took us by surprise. I'm Albert and this is–where is he?–this is Tony, my best friend."

"*Frightfully* pleased to meet you," said the sea serpent. He had rather an affected manner. " My dears, what *is* this place? I seem to have arrived at the ends of the earth! "

" It's Tregunna Cove, in Cornwall. It's our home, and we like it," said Tony sturdily.

The sea serpent shot a quick look at him.

" No offence meant," he said, " I assure you. As a matter of fact I'm most awfully interested to meet you, especially Albert. I never really believed before that there were such things as dragons. I always thought that they were fabulous mon-sters."

Albert was so annoyed that he could feel himself getting red hot, and smoke began to puff out of his nose.

" Fabulous monsters indeed! " he said. " Nothing of the sort. If *anyone* is a fabulous monster, it's you! "

" Here, wait a minute you two before you start

squabbling," said Tony hastily as the two creatures began glaring at each other in a very dangerous way. "What is a fab–fab–what you said monster anyway?"

"It is a creature that doesn't exist, a myth, a fable, a fairy tale," said Albert, "and whatever else I am, I'm not *that!*"

"Well, neither am I," said the sea serpent.

Tony drew Albert aside and whispered in his ear.

"Look here, I think we ought to ask him to come ashore. I mean, he *is* a visitor and we can't be rude to him–hey, look out! You nearly scorched my jersey! Do cool down, Albert. Why on earth are you so cross?"

"I'm *not* cross," said Albert, very crossly indeed. "Ask him ashore if you like. I'm going home."

Tony looked at his friend. The dragon's face was set in hard, sulky lines and he was glowing orange with heat all over. His tail lashed softly and little puffs of smoke kept coming out of his nose.

"Why, Albert!" he exclaimed. "I believe you're jealous of Sidney!"

The dragon gave a high, unnatural laugh.

"Jealous!" he said. "My poor dear Tony, what on earth have I got to be jealous about? You can't

72

really suppose that *I* care *what* you do about that rather common-looking creature who has come pushing his way into our sea? I simply don't notice him, don't notice him at all! " And Albert turned away with great dignity and began climbing the steep path which led up to his cave on the hillside.

Tony gazed after him in astonishment. He had never known his friend to behave like that before! When he turned back to the shore the sea serpent was lying in the shallow water, coiled round and round like a great snake with just his head showing above water. He really was enormous. He was about as thick through in the middle as a very large bull and long enough to go twice round the Bank of England.

The sea serpent looked after Albert's retreating form and then winked at Tony.

" Not very friendly, is he? " he asked. " Bit of the green-eyed monster, I'm afraid, wants to be the only pebble on the beach."

" I don't know what you mean," said Tony. "Albert's eyes aren't green and he isn't a monster."

Sidney giggled, which sent a ripple right down his body in the most interesting way. Tony watched it going round and round all the curves until it got to the tail. " I mean our scaly friend is just plain jealous," said Sidney.

"Well, he says he isn't, and I believe him," said Tony loyally.

"Well, if he isn't jealous, let him prove it."

"All right. But how?"

"Ask him," said Sidney, giggling again, "to come for a swim. Tell him we're going to have a water picnic, all three of us. Say you think it'll be great fun because I'm such an interesting sort of person and you wouldn't miss it for anything."

"What is a water picnic?" asked Tony doubtfully. "If it means going underneath I'm not going to. The water gets up my nose and I feel as if I were going to burst. And Albert doesn't like it either."

"I'll *bet* he doesn't!" said the sea serpent. "But it's all right, you needn't worry. All we'll do is, we'll swim out to that flat rock and lie in the sun and eat—well, anything you like. What *do* you like?"

"Cake," said Tony. "And toffee apples and—"

"Well, that's all right then," Sidney broke in. "You eat those and I'll eat barnacles, and Albert can eat seaweed."

"That's all right for you and Albert," said Tony, "but I haven't *got* any cake."

"Too bad," said the sea serpent absent-mindedly. Tony could see he wasn't really thinking about cake at all. "Now be a good little chap and hop off

75

and fetch Albert back, and then we can make a start."

Tony went slowly up the path to the dragon's cave. He didn't really like Sidney and he didn't want to go for a water picnic, but in a way Sidney was a sort of visitor and he felt he ought to be polite. He said as much to Albert, whom he found huddled grumpily inside the cave.

"Visitor?" said Albert. "Funny sort of visitor! Who asked him to come here I'd like to know. And why does he want us to come for a water picnic? Tell me that."

"I'm sure *I* don't know," said Tony.

"Then I'll tell you. He wants us to come simply and solely so that he can show off. I know his sort! He knows dragons aren't very good in the water—mind you, Tony, I *can* swim, but my style is—well—it's not up to sea serpents' standards, and I shouldn't think yours is either?"

"I can only do breast stroke," said Tony. "And not very fast."

"There you are. I can see it all. You and I, Tony, not at our best in the water and that—that—half-mile of old black hose-pipe swimming circles round us and showing off like mad. I'm not going."

"I think you'll have to come, Albert," said Tony, "or he'll be simply horrid about you. He'll say you're frightened or something. And me too."

"Now wait a minute," said Albert suddenly, holding up a claw for silence. "I've got an idea! Yes—no —yes, I'm sure it would work! And I can do it, I know I can. Oh, what fun!"

"Well, what is it?" asked Tony impatiently.

"I'm going to—no, I don't think I'll tell you, Tony, in case it doesn't come off, but listen now. If I cough, like this—" and Albert gave a cough which nearly blew Tony off his feet, "oh, sorry, old chap, didn't mean to do that—well, when I cough, *swim for the shore* as fast as you can and wait on the beach. Oh, this is going to be good!" And Albert, in high spirits, started off at a great pace down the path to the beach, followed by Tony.

When Sidney saw them coming he uncoiled several yards of his neck and waved.

"Hullo there!" he called. "Coming to my water picnic? That's fine! I expect you're *wonderful* in the water, Albert! I can't wait to see you swimming!" And he laughed in a very ill-mannered way.

"Beast!" muttered Tony furiously in Albert's ear, but Albert only smiled.

"Just wait!" he whispered back. "Now keep behind us, and when I cough, don't forget, make for the beach!"

They started away, Sidney showing off for all he

was worth, swimming in loops and curves, round the others, over them, under them, diving—it really was a wonderful display. Albert plodded on, swimming slowly with his short, stumpy legs, and Tony did his breast stroke and was soon left far behind.

Suddenly Albert coughed.

"Water in the lungs, old chap?" enquired Sidney, smiling in a horrid, superior way. "You shouldn't swim with your mouth open, you know, it's simply asking for trouble, old boy."

Albert didn't reply, but Tony, glancing at his friend before he turned to swim for the beach saw a thin trickle of smoke coming out of the dragon's nose.

" Old Albert's getting warm ! " he thought. " Sure sign he's angry. My word, he must be really upset. Now the *water's* getting warm, it's getting quite hot ! "

He scrambled out of the water on to the beach and stood up to see how the sea serpent was standing the heat. Sidney had stopped showing off and was swimming round in rather an anxious way, panting a little like a dog who is lying in the sun. As Tony watched, Albert swam slowly up to Sidney and looked him straight in the face.

" I'm a patient sort of chap," he said, " but sometimes I take a dislike to somebody, as it might be you, Sidney, and then I get a bit heated."

" Heated ! " said Sidney, " I'll say you do ! The sea's getting quite hot. Here, steady on, I can't stand this, it's nearly boiling. I shall cook in a minute. Cool down, old man, cool down ! "

But Albert, so far from cooling down, began blowing fire and smoke out of his nostrils and all his body glowed fiery red. The sea around them both began to bubble and boil.

" Help ! " panted Sidney. "This is frightful ! This is worse than the tropics ! All right, Albert, you win. You want to get rid of me and you have. I'm off ! " And he began to swim with all his might away from Tregunna Cove and out to the open sea.

Albert roared with laughter, and then, treading water, he put his claws each side of his mouth and yelled:

"Hi! Sidney! Fried Fish! FRIED FISH! FRIED FISH!"

Albert and the Baby Dragon

It was one of the first frosty days of Autumn, when the sun is bright but not hot, and the trees are red and yellow and gold like flames in the sky. Albert the dragon had been out nutting with his friend Tony and was now sitting, tired out but contented, in front of a crackling wood fire eating toasted seaweed and sipping hot elderberry tea. The fire had made him drowsy and he was just nodding off to sleep when he heard a sound that made him sit up in his chair, wide awake in a moment.

The sound came from just outside his cave, and it was exactly like a baby crying!

" It can't be," said Albert to himself. " It must be the wind, or the seagulls."

He listened again and this time he heard the noise quite clearly.

" That's not the wind! " said Albert. " Or the seagulls." He got up and stared uneasily in the direction of his front door.

" If it's a baby," thought Albert, " and I'm sure it

is a baby, and if I go out there and its mother comes along she'll say I made it cry. In fact she'll probably say I was going to eat it and that's why it's crying. I've told these people over and over again that I'm a vegetarian and I never ate a child in my life, but do they believe me? No, they don't. They frighten their poor little children by saying 'the dragon'll eat you if you don't behave!' As if I would!"

He listened again, and again the baby cried, the sad little cry of a baby who is cold, and hungry, and lonely. Albert could bear it no longer.

"I'll have to go and see," he told himself. "I can't leave the poor little thing out there." And stopping only to wrap a scarf round his throat because he was very apt to catch colds, he went over to the door, opened it, and looked out.

He saw, lying on the flat slab of rock where he always sunned himself in fine weather, a woven rush basket with handles to carry it by, and inside the basket, warmly tucked up but crying bitterly lay—a baby *dragon!*

"Good gracious!" exclaimed Albert. "Well! That's not the kind of baby I expected to see! I didn't know any of our chaps in these parts were married, let alone had families! Come to that, I don't know that I've ever seen a baby dragon before!"

He came closer to the basket and peeped in nervously. The baby dragon looked up at him and its tears ceased to flow. It smiled, and Albert, very flattered, smiled back.

"Hullo–er–little chap!" he said. "What are you doing here? Where's your Mummy, eh?"

At the word "Mummy" the baby dragon screwed up its face and began to cry again, louder than before.

"Oh, hush!" implored Albert. "Don't cry, baby! Dear me, what shall I do?"

He tried rocking the basket, but the baby didn't care for this and cried harder than before. It made such a noise that Albert did not hear steps coming up the path to the cave, and started violently when Tony's voice said:

"I say, I left my basket of nuts behind and I've had to come all the way back–goodness, Albert, what *have* you got there?"

"Oh, Tony," said Albert, "I'm so glad you've come! Look at this!"

Tony came and peeped into the basket and then he said in tones of utter astonishment:

"It's a baby dragon!"

"Of course it is," said Albert. "Anyone can see that. The point is, Tony, what is it doing here?"

"Don't you know it then?" asked Tony.

"Of course I don't. I've never seen it before in my life."

"That's queer," said Tony, frowning, and then his face cleared and he said :

"Of course! I know! It's an orphan dragon and it's been left on your doorstep because it's well known you have a kind heart! "

Albert turned quite pale.

"You don't mean that? " he asked anxiously.

"Yes, of course I do, you're known as the kindest-hearted dragon in Cornwall," said Tony.

"No, no, I don't mean about the kind heart! " exclaimed Albert impatiently. "I mean about the baby being left on my doorstep."

"Of course I mean it," said Tony. "Well, here it is, isn't it? And this is your doorstep. You won't deny that, I suppose? "

"No, of course not," said Albert. "You must be right. Someone has heard that I'm a good-natured sort of chap who wouldn't turn a baby from his door. But what am I to do, Tony? I'm just an old bachelor. I don't know the first thing about babies."

"It's a problem," said Tony thoughtfully. "I'll have to think. But I'll tell you what I do think you ought to do, Albert, and that's bring the baby into your cave. It's cold out here, and it's beginning to get dark."

Albert looked anxious.

"Once I bring it in I may never get rid of it again," he said, and then stopped as he saw Tony's horrified expression.

"What a thing to say!" exclaimed Tony in a shocked voice. "Get rid of it indeed! People adopt babies when they find them on their doorsteps, Albert. They don't talk about getting rid of them!"

"Adopt them!" said Albert. "You mean bring them up?"

"Of course. It's always done. You'll get frightfully fond of it, Albert. It will be the joy of your declining years."

"My years aren't declining," said Albert crossly. "I'm quite young as dragons go, not quite a hundred and forty-nine."

"For goodness sake, don't stand there arguing," said Tony. "That baby's hungry. Look how he's chewing his little claw."

"Hungry? Oh dear! I'll give him some of my toasted seaweed. And perhaps you're right, Tony. Perhaps we had better take him in near the fire. I'm beginning to feel a bit shivery myself," said Albert.

"Toasted seaweed!" scoffed Tony. "Don't you know *anything*? Babies are fed on milk."

"But I haven't any milk! Take the other side of the basket, Tony, like a good fellow, and we'll carry him in. There! That's better. Look, he's smiling!

85

He likes the fire. But what are we to do about milk? "

"I'll slip home and get some," suggested Tony. "Mother will have done the milking by now and I can hop into the dairy and get a jugful without being seen."

"Surely she wouldn't grudge a little drop of milk to a baby dragon?" protested Albert, but Tony said:

"Oh, wouldn't she? You know how she hates dragons. She didn't mind you so much until we pinched her feather bed for your Aunt Emmeline, but now she hasn't got a good word to say for you. No, I'll have to take the milk when she isn't looking. I'll get the feeding bottle she uses for orphan lambs too. Cheer up, Albert, don't look so glum! We'll have the baby fed in no time!"

"You are a true friend, Tony," said Albert, laying a claw affectionately on Tony's shoulder. "Cut along home, old chap, and fetch the milk."

When Tony had gone Albert sat down in his chair by the fire and stared at the baby dragon. It was quiet now, soothed by the warmth, and it smiled sleepily at Albert when he bent over the basket.

"It really is rather a dear little thing," thought Albert. "I expect I shall enjoy having it very much when I get used to the idea. After all, it *is* a bit lonely up here all alone and Tony can't be with me all the time. When this little fellow gets a bit older he'll be able to trot around after me, and it will be fun taking him down to the beach when I go seaweeding, and teaching him to fly."

He bent down and carefully tucked the blanket more cosily round the baby's neck.

"There, there!" he said. "I'll take care of you, old fellow! We're going to be great friends, aren't we?"

The baby dragon gurgled and blew a tiny puff of smoke out of his nose. Albert was entranced.

"Clever boy!" he exclaimed. "Oh what a clever little draggy-waggy-waggy!"

"Well, really, Albert!" came Tony's voice from the door. "I never thought you'd get so silly and soppy over a baby!"

Albert started guiltily.

"I was only trying to keep him amused," he said quickly. "Have you got the milk?"

"Yes I have," said Tony. "And the bottle. Didn't I have a job to get it though? Mother keeps it on the kitchen shelf and I had to wait until she went out of the room. I thought she'd never go, so at last I went outside the window and made a noise like a fox chasing the hens. She came out quick enough then, and I ran in and got the bottle."

"Quick thinking!" said Albert approvingly. "Now then, put the milk in the bottle."

"We've got to warm it first," said Tony. "We

always do for the lambs. And we ought to put cod liver oil in it too."

"I haven't got any," said Albert. "And what's more I don't believe it's good for dragons. Nobody ever gave it to me, and look how big and strong I am.

There! now I've warmed the milk. You pour it into the bottle, Tony. Your hand is steadier than mine."

Tony poured the warm milk into the bottle, and the baby dragon must have smelt it, because he began bouncing up and down in his basket and holding his little claws up in the air.

"He wants to be picked up," said Tony. "Go on, Albert."

"What—me?" said Albert in alarm, and Tony said:

"Yes, you. If you're going to adopt this baby you'll have to pick him up sometime, so you may as well start now."

Very carefully Albert lifted the tiny dragon out of the basket, wrapped the blanket more closely round him and sat down again, feeling very nervous.

"Bottle please, Tony," he said, and Tony handed him the bottle of nice, warm milk.

The baby dragon grew violently excited and bounced so hard that Albert nearly dropped him on the floor. He squealed and grunted and puffed smoke out of his nose while Albert tried in vain to put the bottle in his mouth.

"Don't be so silly!" implored Albert. "Look, Baby! Here's your bottle. Stop squealing and take it in your mouth!"

But the baby was by now so excited and puffing out smoke at such a rate that Albert nearly pushed the bottle into his eye, instead of his mouth. The baby began to get cross, and, as you know, when dragons, even baby ones, get cross, they get hot.

"Ow!" said Albert suddenly. "I can't hold him much longer, he's burning me!"

"There's a very nasty smell of scorching," remarked Tony anxiously. " It's his woolly blanket! "

" I – never – knew – babies were – so – difficult,"
panted Albert, throwing the now very hot baby
from claw to claw. " I shall–have to–drop him–in a
minute! "

" Don't do that! " said Tony. " Take him outside! Perhaps he'll cool down in the night air! "

Albert staggered to the door of the cave. The baby
was getting crosser and crosser and hotter and hotter
every minute. He wanted his bottle, and he had been
shown it and then it had disappeared again and he
couldn't understand it at all. So he bawled and wriggled and even tried to bite Albert, and the smell of
scorching grew stronger and his nice white blanket
began to turn pale brown. When he felt the cold
evening air on his face he stopped being cross and
just became plain miserable and he yelled at the top
of his voice!

" Why did I ever let Tony talk me into adopting
this baby? " thought poor Albert despairingly, and
his heart sank as he considered the years ahead, full
of bottles, and with a cross baby being silly about
every single one!

And then, suddenly, something quite unexpected
happened! There was a rush of air and a great flapping of wings, and out of the darkening sky there
descended a large, plump, lady dragon! She simply
snatched the baby out of Albert's arms and then

90

turned on him like a fury, flames darting from her nose and all her scales glowing red with rage!

"Dragon-napper!" she shouted. "Oh, you wicked, wicked wretch!"

"Dragon-napper?" repeated Albert in a dazed sort of way. "But I assure you–I had no intention– I never thought–"

"Then you'd better think now!" snapped the lady dragon, cuddling the baby and glaring at Albert. "It's a nice thing if one can't put one's baby down for five minutes while one goes to gather a few nuts, having come all the way from the Scilly Isles to get them because one's heard the finest nuts in all Cornwall grow round here and one happens to be giving a party! And then, lo and behold! Some horrid wretch dares to steal one's darling child, and not content with stealing it, makes it so cross its best blanket gets all scorched and–"

"Oh, for goodness sake be quiet!" shouted Tony suddenly. It was not at all polite of him but he felt he must do something to help poor Albert, who was so upset he was nearly in tears.

The lady dragon was so surprised that she stopped short and stared at Tony. Then she said:

"Why *should* I stop talking, if I may ask?"

"Because what you're saying isn't true," said Tony sturdily. "Albert isn't a–what you said–at all. He's the kindest-hearted dragon in Cornwall and all he wanted to do was give a poor little orphan dragon a home. You ought to be very grateful to him instead of being so horrid and calling him names, so there!"

The lady dragon seemed quite taken aback. She didn't say anything for a moment, but put the baby in its basket and tucked it up ready to go. At last she said, rather grudgingly:

"Well–we all make mistakes sometimes. If I've said anything I shouldn't, I'm sorry, I'm sure."

Then she picked up the basket in her claws, rose into the air with a great flapping of wings and flew off in the direction of the Scilly Isles.

Albert and Tony watched her until she was out of

sight. Then Albert heaved a sigh and said thoughtfully:

"A pity, in some ways. The little chap would have been company for me. At the same time he seems to have an awful temper, like his Mum. Perhaps, after all, everything has turned out for the best."

Albert's Christmas Party

It was Winter in Cornwall, the coldest Winter anyone could remember. Even Albert, who was nearly a hundred and forty-nine, which is young for a dragon, could only remember one other like it.

"It was when I was quite a little chap," he told his friend Tony as the two of them struggled up the path to Albert's cave through a biting wind. They had been down to the beach, collecting driftwood for Albert's fire and were heavily laden with the pieces of smooth, bleached wood which the sea throws up on to the shore every high tide.

"I bet it wasn't as cold as this," said Tony, rubbing his frozen nose with a red-mittened hand. "My father says it's going to snow, and you know quite well, Albert, it hardly ever snows in Cornwall."

"The year I'm talking about," said Albert, "it snowed and snowed. We youngsters loved it because we could slide and make snow-dragons and so on,

94

but the people in your village, Tony, were in a very poor way. The road was blocked and no one could get in or out and the food began to run short."

"Well, I hope that won't happen this year," said Tony. "It's nearly Christmas, and we don't want to run short of food at Christmas time. What should we do for the party?"

"Is there going to be a party?" said Albert wistfully. "I suppose–but no, of course they won't."

"Who won't what?" asked Tony, and Albert said shyly:

"I suppose they won't invite–me?"

Tony looked at his friend's eager face and felt very uncomfortable. He knew how the people in the village felt about dragons. He had told them over and over again that Albert was a good dragon, and a vegetarian who never, never ate children or did anyone any harm, but they just didn't quite believe him.

"I'm afraid they won't, old chap," he said reluctantly, and Albert sighed.

"Tell me about it, Tony," he said. "Even if I can't go I'd like to know all about it, so that I can imagine what it would be like to be there. Tell me what you do at a party."

"Well," said Tony, "it's being held in my father's big barn, and the barn will be decorated with holly and ivy and mistletoe, and there'll be music and dancing and games, and half-way through we'll have a scrumptious supper, with turkey and plum pudding and mince pies and oranges and nuts and–"

"Stop!" said Albert. "I can't take in any more. It all sounds so wonderful! Oh, Tony, how I wish I could be there!"

"I wish you could too," said Tony. "Poor old Albert! I'll tell you what I'll do! I'll bring you some oranges and nuts and a mince pie if I can get hold of them without being seen."

"Oh, thank you, Tony!" said Albert gratefully. "We could have a little party of our own the next day!"

"You have worried me though," said Tony. "Talking about the snow. You see, the oranges and nuts and things have to come from the market town, and the fiddlers who play for the dancing come from the next village, so if the road is blocked and they can't get through we shan't have any fun at all."

"We must hope for the best," said Albert. "That's all."

But no amount of hoping did any good. Three days before Christmas the sky grew dark and the snow began to fall, lightly at first, then thicker and thicker, until the air was full of whirling flakes and the whole countryside was covered with a deep, pure blanket of white. When Tony woke up next morning he looked out of his window and hardly knew the landscape, it was so different. He was so excited that for the moment he forgot all about the party.

"Snowball fights!" he thought joyously. "Snowmen! Sliding!" He hurried to put on his clothes and dashed downstairs into the kitchen where he found his mother making the porridge for breakfast.

"Oh, Mother!" he exclaimed. "Isn't this fun?"

"Fun!" said his mother, stirring the porridge very hard. "Fun, do you call it? And how do you think we're going to get the goodies for the Christmas party? Road be all blocked with snow and no one can get neither in nor out till it be gone. Fun, you call it!"

Tony ran to the door and looked out. He could

see at once that his mother was right. There was no trace of the road which wandered over the moor to the other villages and the little market town. Tregunna Cove was quite cut off from the outside world!

"This is just like Albert said it was when he was young," said Tony as he realized the disaster. "He says the snow blocked the road until everyone began to get short of food."

"I don't take no account of what dragons say," said Tony's mother. "Pesky great things, they be! But one thing's sure: there'll be no Christmas party the day after tomorrow, for you can't give a party without goodies and music, and we can't get either if the snow don't clear."

Tony sat down to his breakfast feeling very miserable. After breakfast he put on his boots and a warm coat and a scarf and a woolly cap and gloves and went out into the farmyard. He began to make a snowman, but it was no fun at all by himself, and the snow was so deep that none of the boys from the village could get to the farm to play with him. Finally he fetched a broom and tried to sweep a clear path from the house to the cowshed, but the broom was too big for him and the snow was too deep, and he made no headway at all.

"Bother the old snow!" exclaimed Tony crossly. "It's going to spoil everything!"

Suddenly, from far up above him on the hillside, he heard someone calling his name.

"T–ony! T–o–ony!" shouted the voice. "Look –at–ME!"

Tony shaded his eyes with his hand, because the

sun was shining on the snow and dazzling him. He gazed up the path which led to Albert's cave and saw the most extraordinary sight. Albert, his short, stumpy legs stretched straight out before and behind, was tobogganing down the steep, twisty path on his tummy, sending up a shower of powdery snow in front of him as he came!

"Oh, what fun!" thought Tony. "I should like to do that!"

He watched Albert enviously. But just as the dragon reached the very steep turn before the farm gate, disaster struck! He lost his balance, couldn't get round the turn, and shot right off the path and down a bank, ending up in a flurry of legs and wildly thrashing wings and tail.

"Are you hurt?" shouted Tony, and tried to run through the deep snow to help his friend, but to his relief Albert soon struggled to his feet, shook himself violently so that snow flew in all directions, and began to laugh.

"I'm all right!" he said. "I thought, just for a moment, that I'd fractured a wing, but it's nothing, just a bruise. Oh Tony, this is tremendous fun, isn't it?"

"I don't know so much about fun," said Tony. "The road is blocked, and my mother says we shan't be able to have our Christmas party because no one can get out to do the shopping. I think it's mean!" And poor Tony's disappointment was so great that his eyes began to fill with tears.

"I say!" said Albert uncomfortably. "Please don't, old chap! No really, I can't bear to see you so upset."

"You'd be upset too," muttered Tony, dashing his coat sleeve across his eyes to dry them, "if you'd been going to the party and then you couldn't go because there wasn't a party after all."

" I know exactly how you feel," said Albert. "It's just like I've been feeling because I wasn't invited. Awful! Oh, Tony, I do wish there was something I could do to help."

And then a perfectly wonderful idea came into Tony's head! He thought about it and thought again, and the more he thought the better the idea seemed to be.

"Albert! " he said breathlessly. "Can you–can you get hot whenever you want to? "

"I only get hot when I'm cross," said Albert. "As you very well know."

"Well, could you please get cross? " demanded Tony. Albert stared at him in amazement.

"What have I got to get cross about? " he asked in a puzzled voice. "I don't feel a bit cross. I'm having a lovely time tobogganing, and although I'm very sorry about your party, Tony, it only makes me sad, not cross."

"Oh dear! " sighed Tony. "I *do* so want you to get cross! "

"But why? " demanded the bewildered dragon.

"Well, you see," Tony explained, "if you got cross you'd get hot, and flames would shoot out of your nose, like they did when the Knight's horse tickled you in the ribs, and if you got *very* hot, with lots of flames you could–you could melt the snow on the road and then we could go to market and buy the goodies for our Christmas party, and the two fiddlers would be able to come and play for the dancing. Now do you understand?"

Albert gazed at Tony and his eyes were full of admiration.

"Tony, my young friend," he said solemnly, "I always knew you were a bright boy, but I never realized before *how* bright you were! This is genius!"

"It's nothing," said Tony modestly. "I just thought of it. But Albert, will you do it?"

"Of course I will!" said Albert. "Delighted! Er–there is just one small point."

"What's that?"

"Well, somebody will have to make me cross, and at the moment I don't feel in the least cross. Quite the contrary."

Tony thought again, harder than ever. Then suddenly he pointed a finger straight at Albert's face and said:

"Who eats children? Tell me that?"

"Not me, anyway," said Albert. "Don't be silly, Tony."

"Who cheated in the fight with the Knight?" persisted Tony. "Who can't swim as well as that lovely sea serpent? Who? Who? Who?"

"Well, really!" said Albert, and his tail began to

lash gently from side to side, just like a cat's tail does if you tease it. "Well, really!"

"Who was the old silly who built a house and burnt it down?" taunted Tony. "Even the donkey laughed. Ha ha ha!"

"Now that's enough!" said Albert. "I warn you, Tony, I won't stand that sort of talk!" And he began to glow with warmth, while a thin trickle of smoke came out of his nostrils and hung overhead in the frosty air.

"Silly old Albert!" jeered Tony, still pointing a finger and dancing round Albert in the snow. "Call yourself a dragon? Who stole the feather bed?"

"I won't put up with this!" snorted Albert, and now he glowed with heat, and flames shot down his nostrils and melted the snow around him.

"Look, Albert, look!" yelled Tony in triumph, pointing to the melting snow. "Now, quick, while you're still cross—go and melt the road!"

Albert stared at him, and then, suddenly he realized how clever Tony had been. He began to laugh, but Tony said quickly:

"Don't stop being cross! Silly old Albert! Who was called a dragon-napper?"

"That'll do," said Albert quickly. "That always makes me *furious!*" And he stamped off through the

snow to the road, leaving melting snow behind him
as he went.

"Mother!" shouted Tony. "Father! Come and
see what good old Albert's doing! He's clearing the
road, and we shall be able to get to market after
all!"

Albert pranced along the road, still red and glowing with temper. Every time he felt himself cooling
down he only had to mutter 'dragon-napper' to
himself, or 'sea serpent', or 'silly old donkey' and
he began to boil again! All along the road people
came out of their cottages to see what the noise was
about, and when they saw the snow melting and

leaving the road clear and dry, they cheered like anything.

"Good old Albert!" they shouted. "Albert the People's Friend!"

Albert went all the way to the market town and then he turned and came back along the nice, dry road. He wasn't in a temper any more and he felt quite cool again, but he was very happy, because at every cottage he passed the people came

out again and thanked him and praised him for being so clever. And to all of them he said modestly:

"It was nothing, no really, nothing at all. Tony thought of it. It is Tony who you ought to thank."

But they only praised him all the more for being so modest.

When he got back to the farm, Tony and his mother and father were waiting at the gate, smiling all over their faces.

"Well done, Albert!" Tony exclaimed. "I knew you'd do it. And, Albert, I didn't mean a word I said!"

"I'm off to market now," said Tony's father, "to buy all the good things for the party." Then he hesitated and poked Tony's mother in the ribs.

"You ask him," he muttered.

"No, you," she said, and the farmer turned to Albert again and said:

"Will you come to our party, m'dear? You'll be right welcome, won't he, Tony?"

"You bet he will!" said Tony. "Well, Albert, will you come?"

Albert was so overjoyed the tears came into his eyes. He put a claw on Tony's shoulder and looked into his face, but he couldn't speak, he just nodded his head.

What a party that was! Albert sat at the head of the table as the hero of the day, and Tony sat next to him. They had all the delicious things to eat that Tony had told him about, and Albert had a double helping of mince pies and oranges and nuts because he wouldn't eat turkey or ham.

After the meal there was dancing, and then right at the end, the door opened and Tony's father came in dressed as Santa Claus and gave presents to everyone. Albert's present was a pair of scarlet mittens, hastily knitted by Tony's mother, to keep his claws warm in the cold weather. He thought they were the loveliest things he had ever seen in his life. But what made him happiest, and what he thought about most when at last the party was over and he was sleepily getting ready for bed in his cosy cave, was the knowledge that at long last the people of Tregunna Cove were really and truly friends with him and so he would never be a lonely dragon any more.

Printed in Great Britain
by Northumberland Press Limited